KT-450-438

This book belongs to:

_____

Sing our sea shanty!

We need a pirate captain
Before we can depart –
A buccaneer
Who will strike fear
In every sailor's heart.

Are you the pirate captain
To lead our motley band?
Both brave and wise
With burning eyes
And a cutlass in your hand?

Ho diddle-ho and
A hey diddle-hey,
Weigh the anchor,
We sail today.

Hey diddle-hey,
A ho diddle-ho,
Set the sails...
And off we go!

Are You The Pirate Captain?

Ahoy there, first mate Herbie – G.P.J.

Avast ye, young sea dogs Codie and Kyle – G.P.

First published in Great Britain in 2015 by Andersen Press Ltd.,
20 Vauxhall Bridge Road, London SW1V 2SA. This paperback
edition first published in 2016 by Andersen Press Ltd.

1 3 5 7 9 10 8 6 4 2
British Library Cataloguing in Publication Data available.
ISBN 978 1 78344 220 1

Colour separated in Switzerland by Photolitho AG, Zürich.
Printed and bound in Malaysia.

Are You The PIRATE CAPTAIN?

GARETH P. JONES GARRY PARSONS

ANDERSEN PRESS

"This pirate ship be ready,"
hollered First Mate Hugh.
"We've hammered nails, chipped off the snails
and even washed the crew."

"We've **mopped** and **swabbed** and **scrubbed** it.
We've cleaned the crow's nest out.
There's one thing though, before we go,
that we **can't** do without."

"We need a pirate captain
to lead us on this trip."

"To make demands,
shout out commands,
and not take any lip."

Last Sighting of Captain Sid

by First Mate Hugh

"We all recall our last one –
that Scurvy Sea Dog Sid.
Never beaten till he got eaten by that giant squid."

The pirates sat there waiting
till First Mate Hugh cried,

"Look!"

"You see that guy
who's rowing by?
His left hand is a hook!"

"Are **you** the Pirate Captain?
Your hook is quite a sight. Was it a **shark**
that left its mark in some **almighty fight?**"

The man said, "I'm **no pirate**, this here's a **pleasure boat**."

"And what you **took** to be a **hook** is a **hanger** for my **coat**."

The next chap had a parrot.
Hugh yelled, "It must be fate!"

"In fact I'll bet
this pirate's pet
will squawk
'Pieces of eight.'"

"Are you the Pirate Captain?"

"Not at all, young fella.
How **absurd**!
It's clear this bird
is part of my **umbrella**."

Another man came holding
a scroll torn down the fold.

Scurvy Sid's

Gold be in the

"Our missing scrap of treasure map!
It's sure to lead to gold."

"Are you the Pirate Captain -
our map clutched in your fist?"

SHOPPING LIST
2 barrels of grog
sea salt
scurvy soup (2 tins)
~~24 clams and~~
~~3 cockles~~
~~1 big fish~~
hook polish
hammock repair kit
parrot food
barnacle
repellent

"This **ain't no map**,"
replied the chap.
"This here's me
shopping list."

Then in the gloom they spotted
a glistening silver blade,
two gold teeth and underneath
a beard tied in a braid!

"Are you the Pirate Captain?"

"Sadly no, m'hearty.
This pirate gear I'm wearing here
is for a dress-up party."

"But let me help you find one
with **courage, brains**
and heart."

"You'll need one who
will lead your crew
and not just look the part."

"Who got this ship all shipshape? Who organised the crew?
Who mopped the sails, removed the snails?"

Motley Crew's To Do List

1.

Things to Mop

Things to Scrape

"Who? I ask you, who?"

The pirates had the answer.
"We know what we must do.
We've all agreed
the one to lead..."

"... is Pirate Captain Hugh!"

"Yes, Hugh's the Pirate Captain.
He's clever, brave and bold."

"So raise a cheer
for a buccaneer
with a heart
of solid gold."

We've Found a Pirate Captain!

We've found a pirate captain
To give us all commands.
So finally we're off to sea
In search of distant lands.

All hail the pirate captain –
Give him your loyalties.
We cannot fail, as we set sail
Across the seven seas.

Ho diddle-ho and a hey diddle-hey,
Weigh the anchor, we sail today!
Hey diddle hey and a ho diddle-ho,
Hoist the flag... and off we go!